Curious George®

AN ORIGINAL **MAD LIBS®** ADVENTURE

KEEP IT CURIOUS, George

by Grant Baciocco

MAD LIBS
An Imprint of Penguin Random House LLC, New York

Mad Libs format copyright © 2020 by Penguin Random House LLC. All rights reserved.

Concept created by Roger Price & Leonard Stern

© 2020 Universal City Studios LLC. All Rights Reserved.
Curious George and related characters, created by Margret and H. A. Rey, are copyrighted
and registered by Houghton Mifflin Harcourt Publishing Company and used under license.
All rights reserved. All Rights Reserved.

Published by Mad Libs,
an imprint of Penguin Random House LLC, New York.
Manufactured in China.

Visit us online at www.penguinrandomhouse.com.

ISBN 9780593096468
1 3 5 7 9 10 8 6 4 2

MAD LIBS is a registered trademark of Penguin Random House LLC.

THIS BOOK IS FOR:

_____!

AWESOME PERSON

FROM:

_____!

PERSON IN ROOM

Wake up,
Curious _____!
FIRST NAME
There's no time to delay!

Grab your yellow

_____,
ARTICLE OF CLOTHING

it's another curious day!

Where will your curiosity

_____ **you?**
VERB

That, no one can tell.

It could carry you as far as (the) _____.

A PLACE

Wouldn't that be swell?

Or maybe your curious

_____

PART OF THE BODY

will lead you to try

something new . . .

Like being an award-winning

_____

OCCUPATION ...

Who's famous like

_____ , too!
CELEBRITY

The _____ is the limit

NOUN

when you're curious.

It will _____ you

VERB

to extremes.

Maybe you'll even peel that perfect _____
you've only dreamed of in your dreams!

Of course,

some days are more

_____

ADJECTIVE

than others.

And some are

_____ **bizarre.**

ADVERB

**But if you keep curious,
no matter what,
you're sure to _____**
                          VERB
quite far!

So, if your day is boring, and you've done it

_____ times before . . .

NUMBER

Keep curious

and look for

the little _____

PLURAL NOUN

that others may ignore.

Because even the most

_____ **things,**
ADJECTIVE

and people you know too well . . .

Like your bestie, _____,
BEST FRIEND
or dear Aunt _____
FIRST NAME
have new stories they can tell!

And if things

_____ bad,

VERB

And you lose the _____

NOUN

that you had . . .

And everything goes

ka- _____-eee . . .
SILLY WORD

**Then read this book
and say to yourself,**

" _____ !

　　　　　EXCLAMATION

Being curious isn't easy!"

Now pick yourself up,
stand proud as a/an

_____ ,
ANIMAL

and get curious about
the very next thing.

Because you never know

what amazing new

_____

a little curiosity can bring!